BOOK 2

Full Circle
The Return

By
Claudette McLennon

EXPLORA BOOKS

700 – 838 West Hastings St. Vancouver, BC V6C 0A6

www.explorabooks.com

Phone: (604) 330 6795

ISBN: 978-1-997587-51-4 (*Paperback*)
978-1-997587-53-8 (*Hardback*)
978-1-997587-52-1 (*eBook*)

FULL CIRCLE

THE RETURN

*They thought the past was buried
—until she came back to unearth them.*

CLAUDETTE MCLENNON

Dedication

*To my family and friends and in memoriam for
Ver J, Perry P and Phoebe W*

$\mathcal{A}$cknowledgement

I must say a hearty thanks to all my family and friends and support staff. To the persons who love me in spite of my outrageous stories and plots support me anyway, thanks. For my sisters who encourage me especially Norma, Alzie and Janett. For the encouragement from school mates and teachers who makes me feel elevated and push me to continue to live out my dreams to write not for comfort only, but to cause introspection and to challenge conscience and rethink what we think we know. And most of all, for gratitude and love of our creator God, who makes all things possible.

Contents

Preface--ix

Chapter 1--1

Chapter 2--11

Chapter 3--27

Chapter 4--35

Chapter 5--43

Chapter 6--57

Epilogue--67

About the Author--69

Preface

Maryanne Radieux is raped by four high school jocks: Chad Broome (chief of police); Matthew Busch (son of car dealer Reginald Busch); Caldren Forke (son of Congressman Andy Forke) and Griffen Spoolson (son of Bank Manager). Confession from Caldren deemed inadmissible; obtained under duress. They are acquitted which caused a   division in the school and local Catholic community. The boys go off to college on athletic scholarships. Chad Broome and Matthew Busch make it to the majors (NFL). Caldren's knee is shattered the first season of his pro career and it ended and now works as scout for the PRIMOS. Griffen was never drafted. Now years later Maryanne is out for revenge. She's a RN and NP and is sufficiently healed from the trauma and takes to the road as a concierge nurse -flight companion. She is not persuaded (by pal Elizabeth) to let go and let God. She is risking the love of Rutherford Woods her high school sweetheart. She risks losing him. Will she?

Chapter 1

As the plane touched down, she glanced casually around. She was very low keyed on the flight not wanting to draw attention to herself. In fact, she dozed. As the airplane stopped and people started to line the aisle she looked through the window. She moved slowly to disembark. She went through and headed for the bathroom. She substituted her blonde wig for a flaming red one. She put on her dark glasses.

"Well hello Jessica Rabbit," she murmured. She heads outside and hails a cab.

"Tryall Cesare, " she said to the cabbie. She caught him looking at her through the rear view mirror.

"Is this your first time to New Orleans?"

"Uh -uh," she said to discourage conversation.

"If you need to go to the fun spots let me know," he said.

She realized he was just looking for additional work and told him she wasn't sure as yet. However, she accepted his card and thanked him.

"The team stays at that hotel. It's a real high-end place, but rather low keyed if you know what I mean," he said.

She didn't but said, "I got you."

It wasn't a long ride and she and she looked at the meter twenty-one fifty. She gave him twenty-seven dollars and thanked him. She entered the Tryall with its plush carpet and ornate chandelier . She walked towards the front desk and a petite receptionist with a pleasant smile asked her for her reservation. She mentioned what the cabbie said about the team staying at the hotel.

"Oh yes, she said. This is their home when there's a game. Our fighting Conformers!" and she gave a fist pump.

Maryanne laughed. "No need to ask if you are a fan."

"They are really nice, most of them anyway. They are catered to here because of the income they bring here. And, many people visit to get a glimpse of them . Did you come to see them play, because the game is Saturday and there's usually a curfew the night before. But you might see them coming from practice a little later. Enjoy your stay."

Maryanne thanked her and followed the direction to the room but, first asking the concierge directions to the lounge. She wanted to go to the room and take off the heels and stretch her toes. For so long she planned to meet Chad Broome and now she did not feel the anticipation she did previously. She is committed to the pay-back, but couldn't understand her calm. She owed Chad Broome so much. The interesting thing is that many people and even her classmates did not recognize her when she visited her mother. She has to admit that at eighteen she still had some growth left which could alter your features. Plus, the little that the plastic surgeon did, was mostly with her eyes. Anyway, whatever providence that made her unrecognizable was an advantage.

As Maryanne thought about it, she remembered her two visits earlier to Port Charlotte and, that's why she was able to get Congressman Andy

Forke in a compromising situation at Dragon Bay Casino. He was sent complimentary tickets to a burlesque show. The politician in him accepted and, he didn't take his wife but defense attorney Mudd. The show was pretty good; the ladies doing a mild version of the Rockettes high kicking number. After the show they moved to a private VIP lounge. She paid for their drinks and they imbibe freely raising their glasses in salutation. Later, ladies started dancing on stage while others circled the room. She noticed one of the young girls went to talk with Forke and, another to Mudd. Curiously Maryanne walked by and the young girl was straddling him while tickling his ears. Meanwhile Mudd was getting his own lap dance. Both men were flushed. She took pictures of them then called the paparazzi. It couldn't have worked out better if she tried. She wasn't concerned if the alcohol lowered their inhibitions. They could've refused and gone home even if it was an hour away. She borrowed the reception's phone and called 911. Luckily, she left the lounge just before the ruckus broke out between drunken mates and, fists and chairs and, glasses started to fly. So, her call to the cops was opportune.

She was pleased when they were hauled out and the cameras started to flash. Pretty soon WPNX was on the scene. Their disheveled appearance was something they couldn't explain instantly. Too add to that, she sent a roll of negatives to the newspaper and sent copies to the tabloids. Driving to an all-night photo shop to develop the pictures was worth it. The headlines were glorious. Even WPNX got in on it, reporting on the incident. The police confirmed they were there but not involved in the fracas. They were not charged because they were neither disorderly nor behind a wheel even though, they believed they were or had been drinking. Maryanne smiled at the memory . Even now pictures were showing up from all the tabloids. It pleased her he had no comments. Before that he vehemently denied any romantic liaison with anyone at Dragon Bay. So, these 'respectable' married men are now headliners: Dragon Bay Swingers- One headline said A Ride Is A Ride with caricature of him and a lady prone. Just so she ruined his career she released pictures on YouTube with the woman. However , she redacted the eyes to be less recognizable and also sent to other media outlets.

Soon there were calls for his resignation. So, operation The Return started with two bastards- the father Forke alibi provider and the mud-slinging defense attorney. She was sorry if children were caught in it but she did not remember at the time. Well, it was sins of the fathers visiting. Her revenge was not based only on physical harm necessarily but, emotional, psychological, and even financial repercussions. But for the rapists, her first crack would be Chad Broome. He hit her. Him more than anyone else she wanted to destroy. Keeping her fingers crossed she would not have long to wait to serve Chad his just dessert/deserve. She kept up with his social life. He was given a lucrative contract for two years- twenty million for a rookie was great. His initial one-year contract was five million dollars. He had a good manager and he was really talented. and he was rushing eighty yards per game. So, he was undoubtedly talented on the field. He had a way to go before he reached Jim Brown, Vital or Sanders . As competitive as that sport was, for a rookie he was doing well. He scored a touchdown recently and other teams were looking at his potential. Though it was his third year in the majors she still considered him a rookie. He had brash and a big fan club. She was not worried because he had a roving eye. Over the last year his name was linked with two young women, a model and a basketball player.

One thing she determined she didn't want any direct backlash to any woman he was dating. She must realize she escaped a toxic relationship.

Well Jessica Rabbit will be downstairs tonight. She would bait him. A gift of the gods to women, he cannot accept any woman not bowled over by him. Maryanne showered and dressed carefully in a 'lame' dress crossed to create a vee neckline and fastened with a clasp at the waist. As she walked, glimpses of her thighs showed. Eat your heart out Jessica Rabbit, you started it I finish it! She was happy the wig wasn't as red as Jessica's. Her eyelash extensions and contacts gave her a complete cover, she believed. As a nurse she did not believe in extremely high heels, so her heels were about two- two and a half inch high. She is always thinking what if I have to run. Jessica went to the lounge and sat quietly. She could watch those enter with ease. She ordered a light wine Pinot Grigio. She wasn't a drinker and her maximum was two outside her home. Many times, it was laced with excess ice so by the time she drank it , it was more water than wine.. That suited her. Soon some members of the team came in, and of course the 'groupies.' She honestly thought those days were gone but, they were very much alive.

A few men drifted her way but, she found the contents of her glass most engaging and they moved on. She was smiling to herself when someone came up and said," May I join you?' She stiffened. She knew the voice. It was the voice of a thousand nightmares; her nemesis. She swallowed. She had to be calm. She had to be cool. She had to be prepared. She wasn't. Be ready, she prompted herself. You can do this. Heart palpitating, she forced herself to relax and schooled her features. Resentment was a flare bright and flaming and resided with her. She did not have to feign fright, it was natural.

"Oh, my goodness! I didn't see you approach," she said breathlessly.

"You seem miles away. What is a beautiful lady doing here sitting by herself. My eyes found you immediately. This is your first time here isn't it? Or I would've noticed you."

Maryanne smiled. "Yes, this is my first time here."

Someone shouted to Chad. "Who's your friend?" and walked over.

"Man, oh man! How just like you Noah. Turning up at the wrong time," said Chad.

"When you are keeping this beautiful young thing to yourself, I gotta know. Hey gorgeous, he turned to Maryanne, Noah Fences, and bowed.

She smiled "Jessica."

"Just Jessica? he asked.

"Jessica Oneses," she said obligingly.

"Beat it Noah, said Chad laughing. You know the saying three is a crowd?"

"Ouch old buddy! Thought we are buddies."

"We will be as soon as you leave," said Chad smiling.

"Miss Jessica, pleased to meet you. Some guys have all the luck." He slapped Chad on the shoulders and left.

Maryanne yawned. "I am sorry I am not going to be good company because I am so tired."

"Really? I was so looking forward to getting to know you- spend some quality time with you. I am smitten by the whole package."

"You are kind. But I worked for almost two weeks to get this time off. And I thought I'd get away and sleep then walk around New Orleans without Mardi Gras . I want to visit Jackson Square, St. Louis Cathedral-Preservation Hall and of course the infamous Bourbon St. So, tonight

I go to bed early. Sightseeing tomorrow and Saturday. Rest on Sunday-Maybe I'll even watch the football game. Who knows," she said smiling.

"It's early yet, stay awhile. You can go walk in the gardens. Many people will still be dining and, there's a night club and, there's a show. I can escort you there. Your wish is my command," he said affably.

"Wow! What an offer. A rising star from the Conformers as an escort. Aren't you afraid I will get swell headed? So very gallant but, I can't take you up on that offer. I need rest. The way I feel twelve hours would do me fine. But, thank you so very much for the offer."

"It would be an honor and a pleasure to escort you around New Orleans. But if you insist on your rest. Let me walk you to your door."

Maryanne stifled another yawn. "Begging your pardon. It's not the company. I'm just tired."

They walk to the elevator and got on. They got off at the third floor and walked to her room. He inserted the card; the light came on and he opened the door. She thanked him and took the key. She closed the door and hurried to the bathroom to wash her hands where he had touched her. She was a better actress than she credited herself. She kept the nausea in check. She was glad it was night and for the contact lens. He didn't see the resentment in her eyes. Now she just needs some Rolaids to settle her stomach. Shortly she got in her pajamas determined to sleep. She was really going sightseeing. She thought of the movies mimicking Bourbon Street and years when the networks showed the images of the parades and the frolicking. She wanted to participate in the festivities when she was a teenager but not now. Her last year of high school changed all that. Her thoughts were grim. She could've just stabbed him but she only had a straw. She smiled wryly not liking the direction of her thoughts. She rolled over and turned the tv on.

She is no killer. She just wants to maime. She is not averse to causing mayhem. What they did to her was by stealth and brutality and cunning. The dual pain of rape and hit in the eye still had the power to set her teeth on edge. Helen Reddi's Woman came to her mind. Thanks to the therapists and Liz she confronted the pain. And now she can go forward with her plan. Over the years she seldom went to church only when she visited her Jamaican family. She knows everyone- church/Christians touts' forgiveness, that vengeance belongs to the Lord but there's residual anger. Her Jamaican family is not providing its usual peace that she needs. (Liz took her there to heal and was adopted). Why did church have to be remembered now. There're much nicer memories she can dwell on like her goddaughter Zoe Taylor Machado, Liz's daughter. She is a miniature version of her mother, who denies it saying she looks like her grandmother, and twin Zachery Tyler had everything for Zane (his dad). Liz and Zane are doing a great job raising their children but, Liz does not believe that. She said they are spoilt by their father, grandparents and a two-way tie by their godmother and aunts/uncles.

"You are just as bad as the grandparents. But they adopted you right? I must need my head examined to have any expectation you'd be any different. You're family right!" said Liz.

Maryanne laughed out loud. Liz's outrage was not catching Zoe before she reached Maryanne for cover.

"Okay Zoe Taylor your godmother has to go back to work. Your little tushy will be mine then, she said walking away. And some people are supposed to be my friend."

Each time she thinks of her extended family it gives her pleasure. Her mother, Felix and Rutherford have all visited Jamaica and are in love with the island and Liz's family. What is great Rutherford and Zane get along extremely well and that makes Maryanne very happy. She sighed. Oh Rutherford my one true love! I really love you but, I have work to do. Just wait for me. After this year I'll be all yours. She stretched and turned the AC up and burrowed under the comforter. As her exhausted body needs solace, so does her heart and body crave Rutherford. She fell asleep imagining him holding her close while she slept.

Chapter 2

She slept for six hours then woke in the four o'clock bells. Her dream was perforated with Rutherford and nightmare of her rape. The dreams are few and far between but, stress and the encounter with Chad Broome had triggered the nightmare. She turned the tv on and ran into the movie Above The Law. She scrolled again and found Eraser. America is really a violent place she criticized silently. No wonder Canada, Japan, New Zealand and some others banned The Power Rangers from their countries due to their inabilities to resolve conflicts peacefully. She must be getting old. She used to thrill to these movies like Above The Law and Eraser. One thing for sure, Vanessa Wiliams is extremely beautiful. The French roll emphasizes all her best features. She remembered when she said to Arnold you are late and his one word 'traffic.' She thought it was so cool back then. As she surfed the next channel showed her the Expendables with Sly Stallone etal. She was on a roll this early morning.

No comedy? she wondered. Where have all the comedies gone. Well maybe she will listen to music.

Maybe she can find John Denver, Karen Carpenter's I'm On Top Of The World. She turned off the tv and reached for her phone. Yes, she can find something on YouTube. She knows the intrusive Google will track her movements even when the tracker is off. But it doesn't matter; she will dump this when she gets off the plane. She reached for her crossword puzzle but soon feels restless. Well at the back is find a word. Maybe she can do that. Within fifteen minutes she exhausted the page. Then she remembered the praise song Liz always play and clap. It was lively. She pondered the person who did it has a Bible name. She turned the tv to YouTube. Yes, she got it; Every Praise. There was a beautiful video. Good old Youtube favored her. She began to hum and clap. It was really contagious.

Hanging around Liz had changed her hostility towards God and the church. Now she remembered with clarity Liz telling her the story of Joseph. His brothers put him in a pit then sold him into slavery. He worked as a slave, imprisoned because of a lie by his employer's wife. Yet he never dishonored God or compromised his beliefs. Later he was able to save the same brothers and the nation of Israel from starvation. Despite all that happened eventually became second only to the Pharoah. Sometimes honey, our prayers. petition said in earnest and desperate longing is so powerful, when the wrath of God is poured out on that person , you yourself feels sorry for him. Don't underestimate prayer. Don't think God does not see. You will see the reward of the wicked. Don't help him. He doesn't need it. For a while she believed that but, it was almost ten years ago since that fateful day. Felix has since finished college and is a marketing executive. He was young handsome and successful. She was proud of his accomplishment; the skinny acne faced kid is a polished executive. She sighed. Nothing changed for the infamous four. They were living high. She sighed. Her lids start to droop and she falls asleep. This time she woke at 9.30am. This time her dream was of Ford. They were on a sail boat. She was wearing a white one-piece bathing suit that covered just enough. His eyes told her everything she needed to know. Hi gorgeous, he said kissing her. Blue skies, fluffy white clouds floating by, calm sea and Ford's arms? Perfection!

She showered, dressed in blue cargo pants with matching top and went for breakfast. She loves the breakfast and doesn't hold back. Thankfully she eats a full breakfast occasionally or when in Jamaica. A bagel with butter or cream cheese usually suffice with tea or coffee depending on her mood. But, this morning the smorgasbord of breakfast offering was tempting. Well, if she indulges, she will find the gym. She has boiled egg, sausage, bacon, toast, cranberry juice and coffee. Heavens help her she loves bacon and sausage. That's her usual indulgence, but hopes her greedy eye didn't override common sense. She picks up an apple, yogurt and pear to take with her. These foods are wicked! Soon you have two chins, big belly and a big butt. Well, she will be walking, she consoled herself.

She left the hotel at a quarter of eleven for St. Louis Cathedral and Jackson Square -New Orleans City Park and then she will find Bourbon Street. Next day she'll visit the French Quarters with the shops of the colonnade. Well, these are the possibilities anyway. She loves parks so maybe she will visit Louis Armstrong Park as well. She is aware of the multiple cameras along the street which is a blessing and a curse. For what she has in mind for Sunday, she has to be extremely careful. She's going to need more than one disguise. She is sure she can find costumes many places. Popular costumes are the best camouflage and she is hoping people are outrageous enough to wear them outside of Mardi Gras. She let herself absorb the feeling of being in New Orleans. She wants to absorb the sight, smell and the culture which figures so prominently in pictures and stories. She figures the French Quarters is the best place to start according to the flyer she picked up and Google show that St.Louis Cathedral built in 1720's is the oldest Catholic church and overlooks Jackson Square Park. She knows she will not get back early. She hopes the Avia walking sneakers hold up. She cannot afford bad feet, but so far it has worked.

The Cathedral was grand and she could see why it was elevated to minor basilica . She guessed it had a   lot of stories to tell. It was not an original building due to fire and hurricane but, its historical significance is undeniable. The French Quarters also beckoned- a smorgasbord of delight in entertainment , sightseeing, food, and of course the decadent Bourbon Street at night. She gathered the wig in a ponytail and walked leisurely in the square park looking at the organized gardens and manicured shrubs and lawn. Another time, another place she'd wade in the water even to her ankles. She visited with the street performers, the live music, the artistic display on the iron fence. Honestly. she was bushed visiting just the Cathedral and the Square. There was much to do. And the language! Every tongue imaginable. It was a cacophony of voices as hawking, greetings to each other and shouts for children and erstwhile companions.

As shadows lengthened, Maryanne let down her hair. It may be risky but she has to see the infamous nightlife on Bourbon Street. It would be so terrific to have company. Instantly she thought of Ford. She literally pines for the man. It is time like these her resolve is tested on her quest for justice. She loved him so much; she wanted him to be clean of anything she did or would do. Sometimes she had to tell the voice in her head to shut up. Now is not the time or place for such thoughts. She is going to beard Bourbon Street. She hopes she finds a transgender to be friend or hire for a private party. Maryanne realizes she should've done this at the Square with the live performers earlier. She put on a mask and entered the Cozy Spot Siren. Fortunately, a couple vacated a table for two and she slipped in the seat. A mature waitress appears and wipes the table. They talk and Maryanne ordered grilled crayfish with salad and a local beer the waitress recommended. She asked about hiring a "Trans" for a private party; explaining it was a surprise party for her friend joining her tomorrow. Sally was happy to oblige. She looked at Maryanne thinking she could get in big trouble, of persons taking advantage of her. She didn't look the hustler type even though looks are deceiving still, she'd look out for her. She knew many. "Pope" would be milder than the others. What that young thing didn't know that some in that are very aggressive and brash. They may wear a dress but that's where female ended. However, some are genuinely nice like "Pope" Jalena Carlyle. They work out a meeting for Saturday at noon. Pope will meet her at Jackson Square by the art display. He will be in cowboy outfit with a red feather. As a gesture of goodwill a fifty-dollar bill is ripped; a piece for each.

Well Bourbon St was Bourbon Street! There was a juggler, and someone on stilts hopping around. There was three card Charlie. 'Step right up his accomplice shouted. Maryanne watched for a while then moved on. She adjusted a cross-body cloth bag she bought that had purchases she made earlier. She needed quick access to her pepper spray from her pocket. She entered a number of renown spots- Bourbon Heat,

Prohibition and Bourbon Live. They say the music is always good. It was 7 pm and she ordered a virgin pina colada. She didn't want it to seem she was waiting to be picked up so she kept watching the door and her watch as if waiting for someone. Suddenly she wished this was over with. Maybe she is getting cold feet. No, it cannot be; should not be. Breathe, she told herself; just breathe. As she closed her eyes, she became conscious of." Feeling Hot, Hot, Ho"t and the original too!

Subconsciously she started to move. She started to smile, panic over. Thanks to Liz she learned how to dance calypso. She vividly remembers the first time she saw Liz danced it with Zane. She longed to dance like that so Liz taught her. As that one finished, she heard Tiney Winey by Byron Lee and The Dragonaires, and their version of Ragga Ragga. As the music washed over her, her mood shifts. Some Bob Marley music should hit right now and low it did. The Hon Robert Nesta Marley visited. He sang Trench Town Rock, Coming In From The Cold and the iconic One Love. As she enjoyed the music moving to the rhythm she was being observed. She listened to Beres Hammond Tempted To Touch and tears streamed. That is Rutherford's favorite Beres song. At that point she walked out. It is time to return to the hotel. She was lost in thought until she became aware of someone behind her. She quickly crossed the street. There was a tall guy in a mask. She tried to remember the route from this morning. She would take the first street car and worry about getting back to the hotel later. She criss cross the street until she saw a street car and got on it and told the driver to go.

She called the hotel told the concierge where she was and he promised to send a cab there. She was very happy to see the hotel. She paid the cab and hurried in. She thanked the concierge and hurried to her room. That was a long exciting day; perhaps too exciting. Her feet were tired. She did not know what the person was up to. Day time is more secure but night and alone in a strange place, not good. Or maybe she watched too many carnival movies of persons being snatched at the parades. Anyway, that's the end of her night life activities. She will see Jalena aka "Pope" tomorrow at noon- broad day light. She will soak in the tub and order a bottle of wine cooler with cheese and olives in case she is up late. No nuke the cheese and olives. Then she started getting paranoid. What if the person trailed her here? She looked around there's nothing that can be used as a weapon. Then she remembers the coffee pot but, that is not glass. She picks up her heels. Somewhere she read where a woman used her heels to kill a man. Now she is getting morbid.

A knock at the door frightened her. She stifled the scream and tied the terry robe tightly around her. She let the waiter in and watched him. While he placed the glass decanter on the table realized she had the shoe in her hand and smiled.

"Just testing to see if I'll be able to wear it tomorrow," she said smiling.

The waiter nodded and smiled. She closed the door herself. When she believed he was around the corner she examined the door to make sure nothing was stuck in it to prevent it being securely locked. She checked and triple checked the lock; testing by locking and unlocking it. She was satisfied it was secure and not tampered with. However, just in case she put the chair under the lock. She is not taking any chances. She examined the window, closed the curtains. Later she will put the decanter on the window sill just in case.

She slept fitfully that night. She is being chased by a monster in a mask. He had green skin and red eyes. If she's to-do this then panic, paranoia, over-active imagination cannot abide under the same roof. She needs to be clear, focused and dedicated. Whatever she has to do depends on precise execution. She is not exhibiting that now. Worst, she cannot fail. Failure is not an option. She didn't drink the wine cooler rather emptied it in the toilet. That is how extreme she got last night. So, from here on its focus! Focus! Focus! She had the same breakfast as yesterday and went back to Jackson Square. Live music was loud and lots of teens milling around. She wondered about them and what of school. She spotted "Pope" and walked casually towards him. He seemed polite and cordial. She asked his preference for address pet name or other. He shrugged. She told him party was for Sunday and they will be at the Conformers party. He is not required to do anything outrageous, just mingle for maybe an hour or less. Later they move to private quarters for conversation and he's to do a striptease dance. He is to reveal he is a Trans and show his props. He's to have a pair of hand cuffs too. She will be in the bathroom changing in a negligee. She'll enter and will be shocked . When CB finds out he's to run and collects his pay at the front desk. He's to get there by 8 pm. She will be waiting in the lounge.

Maryanne got to the lounge at 7.15 pm. The game went in double overtime. Hopelessly tied, finally Millington scored a field goal and the Conformers won. They are happy to get a win no matter the margin of victory. The coach said they would review the tape and make improvements. Said the Gallentes was a tough team. They would have the victory celebration but should be ready for 8 am practice in the morning. Maryanne is once again Jessica Rabbit. She is wearing an emerald green sheath dress with a slit at the side and the back bare to the waist. It is a beautiful dress and with her hair in a bun she looked elegant. She waited and Pope Jalena Carlyle showed up.

"Hey honey! Slap me why don't you. Honey my splendid siren, you look gorgeous."

"Hi Pope. You are shining. You turn out mighty fine. Didn't see our escort yet. Be impressive; you might get another invite. You never know. So, it's Pope in private but Jalene in public. Do you remember the plan?"

"No worries darling. I got you. I'll be my dazzling amazing self," said Pope.

Simultaneously Chad Broome walked towards them.

"My what a beauty. You look spectacular," he said.

The way his eyes devoured her she felt like a happy meal to a starving child. He kissed her cheek (and she tensed not to flinch) then asked," who is your friend?"

"Oh. This is Jalene," she said.

"Wow! Let me escort you two lovelies ," and offered his arms to both of them. They create a stir as they walk in. That emerald dress promised so much but, would give nothing. Maryanne smiled at the compliments. The guys mill around for introductions . The minutes fly by and she barely caught Pope's eye- head movement. Shortly Chad maneuvers them to the door. Maryanne can see the gleam in his eyes.

"What about us taking the party to my room. Maryanne agreed but said she must collect a package from the front desk. There was an additional piece to her dress she didn't wear as she believed it was too fussy. They took the elevator. Chad's room is on the second floor which suits her. If she has to run or slide through a window the drop would not be too far away. Chad had an array of , whiskey drinks: rum, burgundy, amaretto, and cranberry, Pepsi, pineapple as chasers. Maryanne asked for a pineapple cranberry and a dash of rum. She has no intention of drinking it but they will find out. Pope imbibes freely while Maryanne pretends to take tiny sips.

"So, ladies what are we doing here? We could get right cozy. Us three can par-tee like we just don't care," said Chad.

As they move towards the bedroom Maryanne says she is going to get the negligee from her bag and goes in the bathroom. She tells them to start and she will join them. Pope helps Chad to undress and told him to lie on the bed on his back and she handcuffs him to the bed. He starts a striptease dance and Chad seem to enjoy the show. In the meantime, Maryanne undresses, puts on a big T shirt and cyclist shorts. She packs her bag, on tiptoes, peeps in the bedroom and sees Pope and Chad lock lips duel and she puts her bag outside and, call the journalist Vicenlicous who is in the garden, tells him Chad is with a Trans. Stealthily she opens the door takes off the safety lock. She hears Chad calling for her to come and join. She answered from the bathroom. She flushes the toilet and turns on the pipe on. She hope he gets there soon. At last, she hears the door open and she hurries and sees the journalist taking pictures in rapid fire. She rushes to the sitting room and opens the window. She is getting the hell out of Dodge. She walks along the ledge hoping no one sees her. Heart pounding, she barely balanced on the ledge. The ledge ends abruptly. Can she swing to the next one. What if she falls? Her breathing is shallow and the old panic seems ready to seize her. She inhaled deeply to get calm.

Why did this look so easy in pictures. She cannot fall. She consoles herself it's the second floor. Make the shrubs and break her fall. She could jump and tuck and roll. She starts to laugh then cry at her predicament. She has to stay calm. She will not cry. She is becoming hysterical. She definitely watches too much tv. She should've run past the journalist. She cannot stay on the ledge; She wipes her hands on her shirt and stretches but her legs didn't touch the other ledge. She tried three times. Does that mean she has to tuck and roll? She looked to left and there was a mock balcony. Before she can think she jumps arms outstretched and she grabs the rail. With super effort she pulls herself up and over the rail. Thank goodness the window is open. The room is dark so she waits for her eyes to adjust. There's a sliver of light from under a door. She tips toe across assuming it's the front door. She hears a voice: 'Thank the gods for favor.'

Maryanne screamed and the person screamed too, apparently frightened by her scream. She opened the door and ran in the hallway. People are around and she wondered if she can pose as an onlooker. What if someone recognizes her? She pulled the wig from her head and stuffed it in her waist. The black net on her head she sleeps in. She wants to retrieve her bag. She asked what was going on and was told there was a break-in. No one was hurt. She eased her way through and got her bag. and head for the stairs. She was completely turned around. She was on the other side.

That was a harrowing experience. The whole episode was stressful. She is worn out. She needs rest. She reviewed the plan. It was good but didn't allow for variables. Well, she saw the journalist take pictures. What would the fallout be. How will he feel knowing he was with a man. But that poor man she frightened. She hoped he was okay. Thanks to the dark she cannot be identified. She was all packed and only has her working girl outfit to pack. She is thinking of ditching the green dress but, far from

New Orleans. It cannot look like what it is- a set up. All that adrenalin rush left and she slept. As she stirred the phone rang and it was Pope.

"Honey where did you get to last night. Oh lord the fracas! I am there strutting my stuff when bam a reporter. I was just getting in my routine, so I just posed with the man himself. Then I just shake my boodie for them. I absolutely loved it. I hope I get a center spread and get some movement on my career. Just want to say thanks honey, for everything. Ta ta now."

Pope was flying high. He loved the attention. Crossdresser/ Trans he was happy at the turn of events. Maybe she will get that high later. She wants to see the fall out but it suddenly occurred to her she should get out of Dodge. She showered quickly and made a clean sweep of the room. She looked at any place that housekeeping might not wipe and used tissue. She changed her mind at wiping everywhere. It was less suspicious. She would rather smudge it plus housekeeping will turn off extra lights and tv , clean coffee pot. She will not worry. She went to breakfast. She had coffee and toast and packed her breakfast to take with her- scramble eggs, sausage and bagel, a small apple juice. She went to the rest room and guests were discussing events of previous night. She got the same cabbie back to the airport.

After she checked in, she headed for the bathroom where she transformed her appearance. She changed her wig, contacts, glasses and lipstick. She has to plan more thoroughly and prepare for and make use of contingencies. He next case is Griffen Spoolson. He was never drafted in the NFL, but is employed as a sports announcer on a cable channel GUSN. The last time she saw him on tv he was talking about his show's potential for syndication and hoping it did on the west coast. Well, before that dream comes through, she has work to do. So don't make any big plans yet Griffen. We have a date. There are no children involved so she is glad about that. She will recuperate from this weekend before she tackles Griffen. She must remember to toss the cell phone. When she got home , the newspaper headline blazed with Chad Broome's escapades. It was on all news network and speculation ran the gamut. How long was he doing that, what was his future with the Conformers and will he be traded. Yes, Chad you and your buddies bragged behind the restaurant. Sure, hope you are bragging now! Spoiler alert! The red head Jessica Rabbit is nowhere to be found.

So, Jessica you did marvelous. Now she will have to work out something special for Griffen. But there is still Matt Busch. NFL players will be spooked. It's just a pity both could not be done simultaneously.

She decides to read the master of plots, Robert Ludlum. She needs a unique strategy. No use busting her brain to invent the wheel when there was Ludlum. Her parents used to read him. She is not sure the Bourne Trilogy is good for her. It is too elaborate and combative. What of Gemini Contenders? Maybe that is a possibility. While she pondered this in the next couple of weeks, she learnt that Griffen Spoolson would be on a talk show in Boston an affiliate of WPNY. She would make sure to be there. She sent for tickets and was delighted when she got it. She will definitely be there. A plan began to take shape what if she confronts him? Yes, it would be ambush but, what of it? Today for me, tomorrow for you. She would have to take the risk she causes ruckus. She would get a case for Boston so she just makes one trip besides, she will be in costume. Her rape was and is real. She knows it happened. Confession received under duress or not they are guilty. Greg paid the price for it.

He woke up but he's a shell, has no memory of it. She was mindful each time she visits her mother, visits him and pays someone privately. He just smiles now. There was no information on the hit and run but, to this day believe the Chief had something to do with it.

Maryanne dressed with care the day of the taping- nothing ostentatious. She wore contacts, designer glasses and auburn color wig. During the show the hostess Vanessa Postee did the one-on-one interview with Griffen later, take questions from the audience. One person asked about the Chad Broome incident which he remarked was an unfortunate incident. When pressed if he thought Chad was gay, he denied it emphatically. He knows for a fact because they were boys together and knows what they did. By arrangement she was chosen to ask a question and the set up was perfect.

"Mr. Griffen, this is a two-part question. Back in high school you, Chad Broome, Matthew Busch and Caldren Forke were very good friends. Are you still close?"

Yes, we are for the most part. We have a bond except, less so with Caldren."

"Your final year of high school you were on trial for rape as well as your three friends. Is that why you know Chad Broome is not gay?"

(Drop the mike somebody!) There was a gasp- Oh my and the people covered their mouths, eyes bulging while he looked like a statue, frozen. Then his face suffused with color. He swallowed several times before he croaked:

"What is this? What sort of absurdity is that?" he turned to the hostess.

"Mr. Spoolson I had no idea this question would be asked but, now it has been asked; what do you say?"

"It is lies; all lies. Where did you get that stray from. Are you trying to set me up?"

"Madam, how do you know this?"

"I attended Chelsetta High in Port Charlotte Florida. That's what I know. The raped girl is Maryanne. You cannot deny a trial. It is public record.

"Wild allegations by a paranoid girl. If we raped her, why are we not in jail? I don't have to listen to this."

"You are right, Maryanne shot back. The Chief of police destroyed the evidence. Tell them who the Chief of police is. And tell them to search court documents. And tell them the rest of evidence was thrown out because it was given under duress. And most of all the forensic evidence disappeared. Witness for the prosecutor suffered a hit and run the day of. Tell them!"

At this the audience started to boo and give thumbs down signs. He walked out at that point to the sounds of jeers. As people crowded Maryanne she said, "Go do your research. It's a public record. Just to protect your job interview DA McNabb and see if I lied. It divided the school. The girls sported 'Racoon Eyes' in solidarity with the victim, boycott all sporting activities and the girls attended prom without dates. Go to Chelsetta and you will hear Marcellus say: 'Something is rotten in the state of Denmark. Speak to Dee Parchment of WSBN TV.

Vanessa lost control of the audience though some listened to Maryanne. They picked up cell phones and said it is true. They were acquitted for lack of evidence. Allegations of tampering were made. Vanessa decided to have an impromptu session of persons who were victims of sexual assault, by family member, date or close friend. She got a panel of four and it ranged from age thirteen to thirty-four. The situations were forcible kissing, fondling to rape. Vanessa knew she had to get legal in on this. She would love to run the story. She got her research team to track down the DA. It was helpful there was an interview with the victim. She would like classmates to interview. Of course, the prize would be Maryanne. She doubts she would get the chance. She had a feeling she had already spoken to Maryanne; the controlled tight voice thinly disguised, flaring of the nostrils showed passion. There was an intense way that she spoke and the stance with legs slightly apart, spoke of controlled anger. Vanessa did not push for her name . She knew it was Maryanne who spoke and explosive anger lurking just barely beneath the surface. She hoped she can sell the idea to the network.

Chapter 3

aryanne walked away from the station. There was no sign of Griffen. The untouchable was touched. She was sure many in the audience were already posting on face book. That was a hot forum to debate. She smiled as she remembered how Griffen squirmed. He spluttered as if ready to burst. You did your ill deed and brought it on yourself. If so, innocent why run down the town drunk. What did he have to say that would incriminate you. She had a premonition Vanessa would pursue it. After all this time , the exposure is needed. She is sure they will call and speak with her mother and the rest of the family. Things could not have gone better. Thousands of people will have it on their face book page and it will snowball to the point he becomes a liability to his station. Extra marital affair, children out of wedlock can survive but rape is such a violent ugly word. Feeling satisfied she stopped at a cafe for peppermint tea. She just needs to catch up with Matt Busch. She would see where his team, Sensation is playing next. She will use newspaper and listen sports cast- radio and tv . No one will track her via sites she visits. She bought tabloids, weeklies, and newspapers, The Globe, The Herald and the Sun.

She headed home. She feels strange all this is happening and she discusses with no one. She w ould call her mother. They heard about Chad in Port Charlotte. Many people now are averting their eyes from Bethany Broome but, they have their supporters. Maryanne hinted at the possible inflammatory news on Griffen. When her mother inquired, she admitted to being there but warned her to tell no one. Her mother told her she asked Bethany how Chad was doing and she gave an abrupt fine and hurried away. That pleased Maryanne. Let her provide him with an alibi she thought waspishly. Every dog has its day and very cat its four o'clock. She's not mean; she doesn't have a lot of sympathy for the Mrs. Broomes and Spoolsons of the world. When you uphold your children's wrongs there is nothing in common.

She pored over the papers in her spare time. Sensation's star Matthew 'Retribution' Busch gained popularity as part of the defensive team. You score against him he is coming for you. He tackled hard and gained the pet name 'Retribution.' He was very good at what he did. Maryanne knew without doubt he would be protected. Groupies were going to be scrutinized and anyone new viewed with suspicion. Since she wasn't one, never wanted to be one, it didn't bother her. Besides she had to be more subtle than that. Their next stop Buffalo Bills New York. So far Buffalo is a small town, concentrated and during a game hotels are full. She hoped lady luck will follow. She is going hoping they need people to work temporarily. The team stays at the Calerdos Hotel. She could pose as a new hire. Many times, they hire extras to deal with high volume. Usually, a housekeeper recommends someone mostly at short notice. She decides to put in an application. It seems two house keepers left abruptly. They need people especially for the game. She was hired on the spot. Her interview; Do you know how to clean? said a stressed haggard older woman. She sent her to Mrs. Turnbull to be fitted for a uniform.

Mrs. Turnbull was a pleasant, plump woman with big eyes and dimples.

"What's your name love?"

"Constance Quail ma'am," said Maryanne.

"What a pretty little thing like you doing here? By the looks of you, you could be a model with the figure you have she said pleasantly. Call me Mrs. T . Everyone does. You are coming in when the monsters are coming. You just need to move fast, have plenty of towels, glasses, wipe quickly and cleanly. Assess the condition as you go in, condition of the floor and see how much time you need for vacuuming. Don't leave anything personal on your cart. Always check your supplies. Always have a backup on everything. Learn to ask for help and don't run up and down fetching or you will never get your rooms cleaned and that's important. After that Mrs. T sewed her name to her uniform. She would begin work Wednesday at eleven am.

The match was on Saturday. Wednesday evening the teams will have a friendly game then they will have practice every day for several hours. She knew from experience they have monstrous appetites and was glad she was placed as housekeeper. She had comfortable white sneakers. Her first day was trying but she kept her head. She didn't think she would be working with the visitors. She just wanted access to the hotel and housekeeping would give her the access she needs. She struck up a friendship with Tony waiter/bartender. Sometimes he works as bartender to the different teams. Maryanne asked him if he knows or met the 'Retribution' Matt Busch.

"Are you kidding. We are practically buddies," he laughed.

"What is he like? Is he nice like he would give me his autograph?

"Oh, I'm sure he would. Tell you what, let me arrange it for you before they meet downstairs. You may not be allowed in the lounge area."

"That's okay. I don't want to. I don't like all that - not sophisticated enough, she said laughing. What room is he in?"

"Why?" he asked suspiciously.

"Well, you know we are assigned certain floors and room. What if so meone asks me what I am doing there I'll have a cover story."

"Oh, that's true. Well, he's in the North Tower. You need a special access key to get off the 5th to the 7th floor. But I am sure I can arrange it. If not, I will get you the autograph."

"Thank you, Tony. See yah later. I'll be in housekeeping," she said smiling.

As she turned away the smile left her face. It seems that getting to Matt is going to prove problematic.

She has to regroup. Maybe she can offer to trade with someone. More than likely the veteran housekeepers will get to meet the "celebs" not a newcomer like herself. As she sat morosely in a bucket chair Sueann a veteran housekeeper came over to her. She didn't want company but smiled pleasantly.

"I need someone to work with me in the North Tower. Are you game? Rita is out today and you seem level headed and not wide eyed."

Sueann was in her mid-thirties but was a no-nonsense person. And to be asked to work with her? She was overjoyed she forgot to answer.

"Well?" Sueann prompted.

"Oh yes! Yes of course." Maryanne could not believe her break. She left with Sueann for the North Tower. Sueann told her they would work from opposite end and meet in the middle. The trick was to get as many if not all the rooms cleaned before the team returned. There was a press conference downstairs in the wading room.

"Okay here we go then," said Maryanne.

"Sure. Let's begin. See you later. Anything call me on the radio," sad Sueann.

Maryanne nodded. She could not believe her luck. She knew Matt's room was 515. It was on her list to clean that room. She knocked with a cheerful housekeeping. Getting no response used her key and entered. She left the door open no need to breed suspicion, then, decided to put the cart half way in the room. She hated making beds so she tackled that first. She finished and moved to the next. Rooms very messy she turned the radio to soothe her. This time it was Marty Robbins El Paso. It was such a sad tale. Her dad used to sing it many times. He next 'slob' room Whitney Houston serenaded her The Greatest Love Of All. One she will take the high note. She told herself in her next life she can come back as a singer like Whitney. So engrossed she was in the song she didn't know she was not alone until the voice said:

"You can start now," in a jiffy or

She jumped and said "Oh! I am sorry. I'll be finished in a jiffy or I can come back later."

"No need. I will only dirty it again. He walked in the bathroom. Here is cleaned, the sitting room and only the bed is not made."

She hesitated. "I do not want management to think I am lazy."

"Well, I'll just tell them I asked not to be disturbed beyond changing my towels." sd Matt Busch.

"Okay if you are sure. Thank you and have a great day and game on Saturday, " she said.

Her heart was pounding so she was sure he must hear it. Her tried to tip her but she refused. To soothe his ego, she said she would settle for an autograph instead. '

"Think, when you retire it may be worth a small fortune. The tip would be spent long ago," she said.

He laughed now. "Good thinking- invest for later. I like you. You are different."

She took it and scoot. Lord knows what she'd have to do for that hundred dollar. Now that is a set up. It was easier to build trust, not accepting expensive gifts, not gawking and ingratiating oneself. She told Sueann she met Matt Busch and got his autograph. As they cleaned the other side Maryanne cut the time to fifteen minutes, twenty tops. They left and cleaned the half of the sixth floor. They were back in housekeeping at 3 pm. After half hour break, they went to the Wading Room and to refresh the VIP Lounge. Sueann's direction for these areas do not hurry, shine and buff. And at the same time make yourself invisible. She followed Sueann's lead. She thought on Saturday after the game and press conference the team would get together and that's when she will make her move. She will gather empty liquor bottles and with the help of over-the-counter sleep aide would let it appear he is inebriated.

When Saturday came, she was excited. She worked and did the usual cleaning. It was more relaxed; the team left early and would return late. So, Maryanne got the empty liquor bottles and the sleep aide. As fate would have it the jock, brought two women to his room. When she got to his room, she heard the moans and smacking sounds and slurred speech.

Damn! What would she do with the bottles? Then realization; Matthew made it easier for her. All she had to do was to let the reporter in.. She eased out the room and two of his team members were outside. She reentered the room. They seem tipsy too. They were loud but thankfully it was almost all occupied by the Sensations. Her nerves were taut listening to changes from both inside and outside. It seemed like an eternity before it was quietish outside. The grunts continued unabated inside. She heard Matt say, Do it again. Oh, mira! She was tempted to peep. She didn't need to be a nun to know what was happening.

Chapter 4

She eased back outside and made the call to the journalist. Heavy in her usual disguise wig, glasses, she forgot the name on her uniform. She didn't have time so she turned the uniform inside out and wig that looked like a clown- short and red, a red nose and she felt safe. She let the journalist in and off the fifth floor telling him the room number. Then a hint of mischief prompted her to follow. When the journalist burst into the room the pose and look on Matthew's face was priceless. Maryanne sprinted out. She bumped in someone and kept going. As she near the corner the mop fell off her head. She went to the other end and took the elevator. She ducked in a bathroom taking off wig, nose, glasses, and wrapping them in her uniform. Her spandex catsuit is just fine. She walked to housekeeping. She locked the door and poured cleaning solution on the wig and nose. She dropped them in a plastic bag and took to the garbage. In about four hours the garbage will be hauled. She dressed in   street clothes covering the catsuit just in case. Nondescript clothes you forget a catsuit no. She took a cab to Blue Egg, a second-rate hotel she was staying for the week.

Maryanne was glad that was over. She had to go back tomorrow and feign ignorance. The wear and tear on her nerves would not do. She needed a long rest plus she was missing Rutherford again. She had two warring but equally important passions : to get the rapists and Rutherford. The way she was feeling the others can wait for now, Caldren, the Chief, the Judge, the Seniors Busch and Spoolson. Maryanne prayed she would sleep despite the hectic and overwhelming night. Oh, Matthew, you made it so easy for me. I didn't have to contrive a situation. She felt good she didn't have to use the sleep aide and she feels better. Matthew provided his own ammunition and participated in his own destruction. You brought two women. The surprise on your face mirrored Chad Broome. She wondered again if anyone would make the connection of the events and the rape.. Maybe it's her overactive imagination working.. Pope presented her a wonderful alibi she was locked in the bathroom, afraid if recognized would lose her job. Thank you, Lord, for my safety she whispered and fell asleep.

He not only makes move on the field but makes move in the bedroom; followed the caption CAUGHT.

The newspaper headlines jumped out at her. He set the scenario she just capitalized on it. She hurried in quite agog with shock and curiosity. Housekeeping was buzzing with the news. She joined in the speculation. NO one mentioned anyone in semi clown outfit. She kept shaking her as if in disbelief. The newspaper was there for all to see. She read the ftirst paragraph and see the journalist got a tip. There was the thought that he is free to form whatever association he liked. No problem among consulting adults Plus his privacy was violated. She had regrets for the girls and have to be more conscientious to keep others from getting in the crossfire.

Sueann decided they would start on the sixth floor and work downwards. They worked the whole floor and by 1.30 pm was on the fifth floor. Maryanne was timid. She was afraid. What if she was accosted about what she knew of incident. What ifs were driving her crazy. Guilt is in deed a gigantic load. So how did the four feel after raping her. No guilt or remorse? Look at her how badly she felt for the two ladies. She has no quarrel with them. Some people are devoid of conscience. Didn't they brag behind the restaurant weeks after? She just has to steel herself and work. She summoned energy to clean. With super human effort knocked on Matt's door. She was hoping to hear go away. After the second knock she entered and ran in him. She apologized for disturbing him looking down not meeting his eyes. She could return later.

"I'm sorry he said. I am in a foul mood and it's not your fault. Leave the bed. See to the bathroom; Just change the towels etc," said Matthew.

Right away she scurried to the bathroom. She put on her gloves and got the cleaning supplies. She washed the bath, basin and bowl. She changed the towels and wiped the mirror.

her voice trailed off

" I will take the garbage from the sitting area and wipe her voice trailed off. He wasn't listening. He waved her off. But she collected the trash, wipe the water mark and sticky stuff off and shot out of there, She almost made it until his voice stopped her.

"What are they saying about me?" he growled.

"Excuse me .Who are you talking about?" she prevaricated.

"Oh, don't play innocent or naive. You must've heard what happened last night and saw the newspaper."

"Oh that. I am sorry sir. I had quite forgotten about that. But if your team mates support you then, something else will take its place. Something else will grab the headlines," she said."

He grunted and this time she bolted. She went to housekeeping and Sueann was there already

her feet up. Maryanne told her to go ahead but did not know she would be held up.

"Well how was it. I said I would give you three more minutes, thenI'd go look for you," said Sueann.

"He was in a mood, scowling and granting. He wanted to know what people were saying about him. I told him to forget about it; that something else bigger will come up , grab the headline and people will forget him. Plus, he has team mates as support. He wanted me to only change the towels but I removed the garbage and I did," she said.

Other staff came in and are discussing Matthew. Many comments were ribald down right offensive and crossed the line. She never liked trashy behavior so she walked out.

"Too hot for you missy? It is life my girl ," someone shouted.

"Cut it Peg. Not everyone likes your coarse talk."

"So why are you still here," Peg asked the speaker.

 "We know you- That you do not know better. You don't bring up right or your mouth wouldn't be from the gutter."

"Bozo! Shut the blank up . You are not the boss of me. You and your little bourgeo friend can go take a hike."

Maryanne turned to flash Peg then changed her mind. She smiled and shook herself. Even the dull and ignorant they too have their story. Peg is hoping for a confrontation but she is going to disappoint her. She remembers Marley's Two Little Birds and   began to hum. She couldn't remember the words but believed if she concentrated enough would forget Peg and she did. She made most of the words but since Bob wouldn't hear it wouldn't hurt him, she thought, smiling to herself. She wished she was at Dunns River Falls and would later go to Scorches for jerk food. She missed Liz and Zoe. In her heart she heard Zoe calling her and could feel her arms around her neck as she hugged her. With that Ford floats in her view. And she was in his arms and that dreamy far away look is reflected in her eyes. She closed her eyes to blot out Ford's face as if that could. After this trip she is going to find him.

That ravenous appetie that plagues her is for Rutherford Wood not to payback the bastards that raped her. She let that thing consume her but no more. Lord please don't let me start tearing up. Truly abscence makes the heart grow fonder. She cannot miss Rutherford anymore that she does. She would work tomorrow then go home. She doen't know why she is bothering because she may never get that pay check. She's brought back to the present by Sueann.

"I like your style kid. You know how to walk away from trouble. Peg can be a real pain in the behind at times. But one day will tangle with the wrong person and, I hope and they give her a good whopping." she said with feelings.

"I will choose my own battle. The Pegs of the world do not dictate to me when to fight. Been there done that! It's like a chihuahua barking at a German shepherd. I am me not someone else. What else are we doing?"

"We are going to clean Ballroom 11, dust vacuum, and rearrange the pedestal stations. Mrs. T knows I like to decorate. When I leave here, I want to do like decorations for christenings, sweet sixteen, graduations or any functions of that sort."

"What about weddings?"

That may come later. You need more for weddings even though I love making bouquets I don't feel I master the craft yet, but small floral arrangements I can do. I would like to have big potted plants that I can use to enhance a room. Girl I have plans. That is why I usually work alone so I can move up someday. If management see I show initiative may be they will consider me. But sometimes I'm torn. I want to have a business of my own but, it takes a lot of money to start. Sometimes I do a double and sometimes a guest leaves me a twenty. One day I found a hundred dollars in the envelope, I got to recetion and asked them to call him, Lucky his fligt was delayed and he said it was no accident, thanks for my honesty. That week I had hefty tips thanks to that man."

"I sincerely hope you start that business. That honesty will pay forward. I really wish you well."

Sueann then revealed a clear box with clear orbs which she placed small birds on a pillar with a beautiful background. They were beautiful and Maryanne said so. Sueann thanked her. They are placed on mint and white doilies Sueanne must have made. She is really talented.

"I know we just met but you are so talented. Look at these. I know your floral arrangement must be spectacular. When you make things take a picture. It can be a catalog one day for your work. For family and friend let them pay for the material without additional cost so you build your business. Give yourself a name; print business cards Florals by Sueann and copy right your designs," said Maryanne.

"I can't copy right. That cost so I can't do it," said Sueann.

"Yes you can. Do poor man copy right. Make copies and mail to yourself. Note the date and do not open it. Thats poor man copy right. If someone steals your designs take the sealed envelope to court. That's your proof. That is poor man's copy right.

Sueann laughs. "Are you kidding me?"

"No, straight up! You have a winner. Don't wait too long to start. Whatever you make for people put small discreet labels with your name and phone number so others can place orders. The store can come later."

"I guess that's why I like you. You are smart and progressive. What about you?" she asked.

"My passion is nursing. Maybe one day you see me escorting one of the old wealth gentlemen. I will do that until I settle down," said Maryanne.

"That is neat; seeing the world while working. Good luck honey. God bless you. Know you were different," Sueann said.

They are friends now but, for Maryanne too short. After tomorrow she will not see Sueann but will miss her as a friend. But she desires to be with her high school sweet heart. At moments of crisis, she misses him the most. She realizes he spells stability, safety and reliance. Pretty thoughts don't help. She is going home. Where is home? What is home for her and a picture pops in her heart and vision; Rutherford Jay Wood. They have been apart too long. She believed by the time they were established in their careers they'd be like some old married couple. They would have two children or so now she's not even sure she wants kid. The only part that survive that plan is her love for Rutherford.

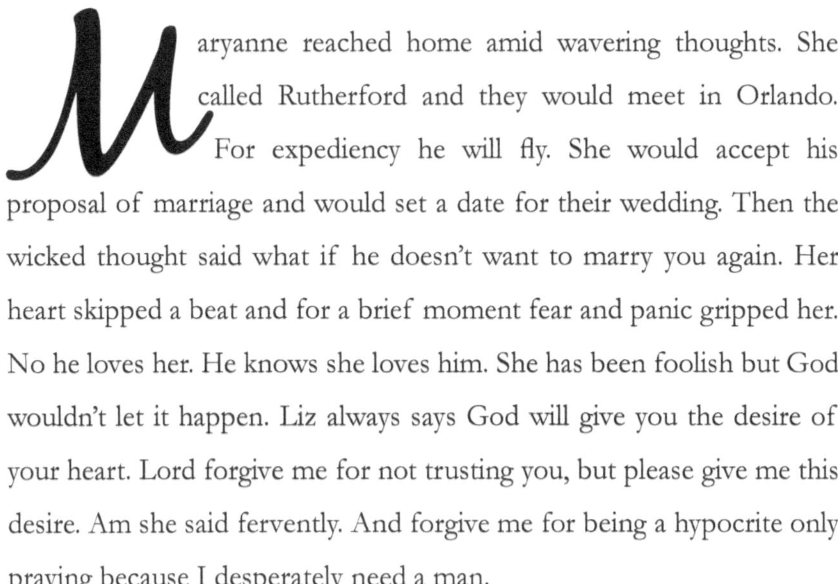

Chapter 5

Maryanne reached home amid wavering thoughts. She called Rutherford and they would meet in Orlando. For expediency he will fly. She would accept his proposal of marriage and would set a date for their wedding. Then the wicked thought said what if he doesn't want to marry you again. Her heart skipped a beat and for a brief moment fear and panic gripped her. No he loves her. He knows she loves him. She has been foolish but God wouldn't let it happen. Liz always says God will give you the desire of your heart. Lord forgive me for not trusting you, but please give me this desire. Am she said fervently. And forgive me for being a hypocrite only praying because I desperately need a man.

The weekend could not come fast enough. She shopped, washed and cleaned. She sprayed the house with air freshener. She baked an apple cake. There's nothing life fresh baked cakes/ pastries to give a house vitality and say home. She is not working and has simple plans for the weekend; either Madame Tussauds, Lake Eda Park, Icon Park-Discovery Park. To her it's a toss between Madame Tussauds or Discovery Park. Ford is on a 4 o'clock flight and she still doesn't know if he is renting a car. She is going to wait for confirmation the flight is on time before she decides if she will pick him up. Nothing must go wrong. She is planning to wow him with Jamaican cuisine. She is cooking oxtail and jerk chicken. Once confirmed he is aboard she tells him she is picking him up Baggage Claim Level two. She put finishing touches to the house, cut flowers and candles. She must create an ambience of intimacy and romance. She is not hiding anymore.

As the time drew near for Ford's arrival, she became very happy. She started for the airport excited like a kid on Christmas morning. They may not go anywhere tomorrow but that would be alright too. She will let him choose. She turned on CBS radio and Journey's Open Arms filled the car and it reached deep down. She loved that song. Was it prophetic? It's in top five of love songs of all times. As she listened the tears form and roll down.

'So now I come to you with open arms

nothing to hide, believe what I say

So here I am with open arms

Hoping you'll see what your love means to me

Open arms

She sang as she cried. The ballad reached her. She forgot the perfectly made-up face. Thankfully Mary Kay mascara does not run. She dabbed her eye and cheeks . Make up intact, thanks M Kay. She wants so badly what is expressed in those words. She pulled up to Level A. She flipped the visor, took out her compact to dab mineral powder to remove every visage of tears. She saw him emerge and her heart did a somersault. He was so big and handsome- no flab or fat. His shirt was flat across his chest and sleeves folded back to his elbow and trim waist made her inhale sharply. His lower muscular legs are covered in navy blue pants. He was beautiful! She got out and hugged him tightly.

He chuckled and said , "I can't kiss you if you have your head buried."

She lifted her head and he kissed her. In her vulnerable state she isn't sure if that kiss was such a good idea. She felt shaken.

"Oh Ford!" she said looking up at him. And he kissed her nose. Thank heavens! She would not survive another kiss like that.

"So, if you kids can move it along home," said a voice of gentle reprove.

Oh! said Maryanne moving to the driver's side. The elder guard had a twinkle in his eyes as he smiled. She waved to him. Well, she has the gorgeous man all to herself.

"How's Grams?"

"She is fine. Wants to know when you are coming to see her."

"Me? What about you? Maybe that's what she asked you and you are flipping it?" she said.

"Now why would I do a thing like that. I am an honest guy," he said smiling; his teeth gleaming against his tanned skin.

"Sure, you are," she said.

"Look at this face Doesn't it say honesty. I am wounded," he said.

"You'll get over it but, I'm extremely happy you are here, she said. And she turned to look at him and he kissed her. And for a moment lost her head, thankful there's no oncoming traffic. Rutherford Wood what are you doing?" she asked righting the car.

"Just kissing the girl, I love more than life itself. Who doesn't know how much I need her," he said unrepentantly.

"She loves you too and, she will prove that," she said softly.

"Pull over," he said gruffly deeply affected by what she said.

"Not on your life. I want to be able to drive home and get there safely," she said. And with that she stepped on the gas eating up the miles. She smiled as she drove.

"Okay M A drive on. That suits me fine."

He eased the seat back to be more comfortable . He fiddled with the radio.

"I am looking for one of my girlfriends Dolly Parton. You see her? Don't answer that," he said smiling.

"Do you think you can just order her on the radio?' asked Maryanne.

"Well, she should know I would like her to ride with me. What about Barbara Streisand? Not here either! he said..

"Do you know you haven't changed music wise? You always love older mature women." said Maryanne.

"Well, they are more dependable except for maybe Whitney H. What do you expect. I grew up with my grandmother. I listened to what she listened until my teens but they are still my roots," said he.

Maryanne laughed. "It's the same old story. Alright I will ask Whitney to stop by here. I have a mixed disc. Here is Whitney singing I Wanna Dance With Somebody," said Maryanne.

As the music hit the air he started singing with it. A series of Whitney songs followed. As the car ate up the miles, her mind flashed back over the events of the Buffalo affair. She wondered if the infamous four would see the connection. No, they are too arrogant and never accepted they were wrong. Griffen Spoolson lost a lot of sponsors for his show and was being canceled after this sesson. Many car companies withdrew as well as sneaker companies. His clothing line Fenspool went down as well. Many other watch dog groups joined the furor. She was concerned for Caldren Forke. He might make the connection. Then there are others to thank: Seniors Busch, the Chief and the banker.

She jumped when Rutherford said, "Where did you go? You did not hear a word I said for the last couple of minutes or so."

"Sorry. What did you say?" she asked contritely.

"I said I am planning to take a romantic trip for two. Are you interested?" he asked.

"Of course! Is that Hawaii or Italy?" she said hopefully.

Rutherford laughed. "Are you planning this trip or am I the one doing so?"

"Alright ! I temper my enthusiasm if you are going to be like that. Where to? "she said.

"The Amazon Basin or the Galapagos Island, "he said .

She bit back. She almost said you gotta be kidding but instead said when she was younger, she wanted to go. The myriads of birds, the vegetation and thousands of animals and fishery left her intrigued. Now conservationists are worried about losing too many animals and plant life and the rainforest to climate change and deforestation.

"Thanks darling, I will fly over instead," she finished.

Rutherford laughed :Really now! Just a pity. It would've been a great trip for you. Guess I might have to find another person to accompany me ," he shrugged.

"Really Rutherford! Really? So what, you are thinking of relocating?" she asked.

"No. Why? he asked.

"Taking someone else would you? And come back to live where? You are funny. Let me see, and touched his forehead. Not so sure but you must be running a fever," she said with emphasis.

"What! Are you jealous my sweetie?" he asked with glee.

"Why? Do I look jealous to you," she challenged.

"No, you are right. ; You don't look jealous; you sound jealous. And by the flashing eyes, grip on the steering I sort of think you wished it was my neck," he said massaging his throat.

Maryanne burst out laughing. "Hold that thought and you'll live a long successful life," she promised.

They finished their journey. He elected to shower. While he showered, she warmed the jerk chicken. oxtail and rice and peas. She rinsed the wine glasses and popped some ice and poured the Muscato Rose. She straightened to see Ford watching her through lowered lids. Goodness the man was a hunk. Her heart stuck in her throat, She couldn't breathe. I need help. Was there ever a man so gorgeous? He was Clarke Gable, Errol Flynn and Steve Reeves wrapped up in one. She inhaled deeply. He better not change his mind about marrying her. This deep lust must find an outlet soon. She must need her head examined. But deep down she knew love was there. She really needed baptism. He was a Viking. He wore a white shirt buttoned only at the waist and the bare chest was tantalizing. In slow motion she handed him a glass.

"Salud!" he said and took a sip. There is something else I'd rather sip and he removed her glass from lifeless fingers. And he kissed her. Now she is drowning. She missed him too much to protest. It was a long time before he lifted his head.

"I needed that. he said hugging her and kissing her forehead. They ate by candle light with both Ms. Gladys Knight and Barbara Streisand serenading. They ate in companionable silence. He complimented her cooking skills.

"Wow M A! Didn't know you could cook this well? What's the saying? You put your foot in it. Yeah. Meal irie daughter.

"Thank you ," she said bowing.

"Irie daughter," he said

"No problem man! Know how it go. A cool runnings!" she said and they both laugh at themselves.

The dishes cleaned the couple moved to the living room where the music was still low. He asked about her goddaughter Zoe. She said she was fine her favorite question being when are you coming to see me. She doesn't understand I have to work. I get no help from Liz excehairpt; you spoil her deal with it. He wanted to know if she did. She admitted it but Zoe is loving. She would ask if she was tired, she will make a bath for me, she'd brush my, hair and put my head in her lap, cover me up so I can sleep. Rutherford was surprised she did all that.

"Do you know I didn't know I could love a child so much until I met Zoe," she said

"Now you can love your own," he said.

As she made to get up he said, "Oh no." He pulled her back. How long M A? Cold shower should not be a way of life; at least not for me. As I thought about this weekend I decided I'd ask you one more time to marry me. I don't want to be standing in the corner anymore. I love you too much for that. I've loved you so long it will be a life altering adjustment if I am not loving you," Rutherford said.

Maryanne looked at him and beamed. Thank you Lord he still loves me she said inwardly. She was so happy at his words she launched into his arms and kissed him. He took over after that. Some twenty miutes later she shifted in his arms. Her heart was singing "Mi amore."

"What were you going to ask me?' she said.

"Maryanne Radieux will you marry me and take me out of your misery? Make me the happiest man in the world?"

"Let me think about it for five minutes. She closed her eyes then said, Yes , yes. Oh Ford I love you."

"It's about time," he said kissing her. They stayed close for a long time. Eventually she stirred.

"I guess we have to tell the family we are getting married. It is going to be a lot of work."

"Why dont we elope. That takes care of the planning and panic."

"You are not being helpful. Can you see my mother's face, Liz and Grams. Ford what if."

"Stop right there. The acceptance of my proposal is written in stone. You cannot backout. We are getting married. I don't care if it's two or twenty two present as long as you are. I have waited a long time. Ask your sister to help you. Kowing her she planned it years ago." he ended.

"What are you talking about?"

"Who do you think I'm talking about Liz/ though she may be mad at you. But you have all of two weeks before we get married, " he said complacently.

"Are you out of you mind" said Maryanne.

"Truth is I should be in the nut house. Yes, I'm mad for you, madly in love with you, mad to wait patiently for your love for you to love me back. Yes I am mad to love you more than I lo ve myself. And just for security I have a back up. Here, listen."

Maryanne was shocked! All their murmurings, whispers of love, their moaning and finally asking her to marry him and her acceptance. Every word on tape.

She swiped at him. "You no good rascal, cheat and ". He caught her hand and kissed her. He tumbled her on the futon wrapping her arms around his neck. They stayed like that. Later she told him she cannot believe he taped them. He assured her it was for saving her. She disputed that telling him to stay away from her. (She was wrapped in his arms).

"I was going to tell you, you have something on your face," he murmured.

"What? "

And the rest was lost as his mouth covered hers. They had both waited too long. It was a dry hot season, a desert of longing, waiting and wilting. And as they clung together that night on the futon each knew the drought was over and there was spring time. And all the emotions held in check for years gushed forth in a timeless song of giving and receiving; of deprived love, release and desire. Two bodies long constrained of the release of love and desire could meld in joy. It was pure raw desire tethering on a fantasy each held of the other. A knowing but not knowing. It was honest, pure, rich, clean love cherished together, and apart. And the invisible barrier broke and they were free to love. A rebirth of love so effervescent, free flowing caught in truth; an enduring love that stood the test of time.

Next morning they woke in shared remembrance. Their path to true love defined irrevocably and there was no going back. Yet they didn't cross the line but they discovered an enduring love. Now she knows she can never live without him. They were united last night beyond the physical. As they had breakfast they chose to go Lake Eola Park. It was tranquil and peaceful. They walked around the lake, had lunch at The Grill and hiked the trail. It was a beautiful four hours, at home they had kebab-shrimp, chicken, peppers, mushroom and chicken and roast corn. She used her kettle grill. Later they compromised on the wedding date courtesy of Liz June 14. Three months and no more. It will be a destination wedding in Jamaica. Liz and Maryanne will work everything out. She will do minimum visits there. The colors had to be finalized with her mother, Renee and Yolande. Grams would need a passport. She is happy for them. Rutherford believes she's more excited to go Jamaica. Ford revealed his parents live in California but no relationship- It end when she promised to come for him at age six and she didn't. She visited twice and; it wasn't ever a goodtime for him to visit them. He has a brother. He tried with his brother and he gave up. He promised to tell them about the wedding.

Because she is getting married, she is slowing her activities but, she is going after Caldren Forke. She found out when he was not recruiting for his old team PRIMOS; he is a motivational speaker for high schools. He encourages abstinence from alcohol, drugs and smoking. He builds after school centers and has volunteers and other run the centers. The centers are equipped with recreational equipment, tools for learning and paid tutors in all subjects. Reports are higher graduation rate and fewer drop outs and, enrollment in college is going up. She visited some of his classes and they are pretty good. She introduced herself student at Missouri State Genave Brewe doing article on athletes that give back and she heard about him. She asked about high school college and recruiting. He was reluctant discussing high school and his friends. He is not friends with high school mates because not in the league due to his busted knee.

He was happy to dicuss the after school program. Passion because one wrong choice impact you forever sometimes. He encourages independence and seek good role models. Obey your parents and know right from wrong. Your heart will tell you when things are wrong. If nothing to do go to church. It is safe there. She remarked about a somberness about him which he acknowledged. She surmised something impacted him? Said he wronged someone and it haunts him. He did not apologize . Although he didn't do what his friends thought he did but he was there, complicit. She asked why not admit and apologize. It was not easy because others are involved. She told him he needs to secure his own soul above the glory of Rome. It seems he has a conscience. My adopted sister always says the sinner's prayer is Psalm 51. I leave that with you. There is some decency in you. You are forgiven.

Maryanne walked away. The anger she felt towards Caldren seem to dissipate. What a revelation. He was 'beat up' by his misdeed, his teenage crime. He was the worst for wear. Here he is trying to exorcise his demons. May be if more men suffered pangs of conscience there would be less crime. So, she wrote the article A 'FOOTBALLER' gives back Caldren Forke. It was ready for print so she substituted hers for NegressTubbs. Not personal Negress just necessity as she destroys the copy. Maryanne flew back to Orlando a subdued person, less thirsty for revenge. It didn't help he canceled their weekend going to some hush conference in DC. He told her she wouldn't miss him as she was fine tuning wedding plans. He said he will call back 8.30 pm. She wondered if he was tricking her and would pop in. He called and shortly after the doorbell rang. She answered him and looked through the peep hole. It was Liz. She screamed, opened the door and hugged Liz. As they talked Liz asked about the phone in her hand. She told Rutherford Liz is there. He chuckled. He knew she would not miss him and hung up.

They had a good time catching up. Tomorrow was for wedding plans. She wanted to hear everything about the family especially Zoe. Liz hands her a letter from Zoe. They talked way into the night. Neither one called spouse or fiancé. And neither of the men expected them to. Both men spoke at 8.45 pm. Next morning the friends had breakfast and went over the menu- appetizers and entrees- sides. Zane and Ford will do the liquor. The bride's maid and chief have one more fitting, the strawberry and butter were fine colors. Liz asked if they decided where they would live. Maryanne said he wants to go back to Port Charlotte or Punta Gorda but has no decision as yet. Early afternoon she called Zane and Maryanne called Rutherford. They talked for a while. Liz wanted to know how Ethan was doing with swimming. Maryanne hung up from Ford so she could talk with Zoe. Liz shook her head and said nothing. Soon it was time for Liz to go.

After Liz left Maryanne wondered what Ford was doing in DC. She remembered he told /explained "Cold Case Files". Theirs case was one. It was assigned to the specialized team/unit and they were working with passion and purpose to find answers. Everything will be scrutinized as well as personnel from the janitor up. Everything will be dissected. They are digging for forensic evidence since it was mixed up, the evidence room will be scoured as the lab where DNA was processed. Rutherford will work on the forensic end under cameras and observers. Everything will be brought to him. He will collect nothing. She is somewhat optimistic. But considering the fall out on Griffen and, lost job and revenue, Matthew and Chad with lost multiple endorsements and trades or expulsion not bad for one person team. She felt for Caldren and was glad she did the article for Missouri State University. May be later he looks and will hear you are forgiven. She is not finished yet. Her next stop will be the mothers. They always celebrate Memorial Day. Port Charlotte you have a visit.

Chapter 6

Maryanne went as a volunteer for the Memorial Day celebration. She will have all her props and disguises. Each year the principals; Bethany Broome, Erica Spoolson, Mazine Busch and Gretchen Forke have done the play The Grand D Day Assault. Her mission is to sabatage. She volunteered with decorating, gluing, and pasting. She set up tables and chairs and streamers. She made herself indispensible doing everything so when it came time for the principals' hopefully, she would be accepted. Because of her deftness with needle and thread ithey send her to help with the costumes for the play. The way the ladies fussed and carried on. Once they knew her name it was Juliane do this, take this in, lengthen this. They are so nauseating she thought. Bethany Broome wanted the bodice adjusted, when all she needed to do was to lose a couple pound she thought waspishly. Maizine Busch needed to do squats to tighten and give definition to her derriere she thought uncharitably. Her waist was too big and she was straight from her shoulder to her heel. She wanted another layer of crinoline. She did not hate them but found them cloying. Mrs. Forke had a nice figure but, her nasal tone annoyed her. Maryanne laughed at herself. Her description is way out. Erica Spoolson bust defied reason. The two breast are lumped into one. These were a challenge to tape measures everywhere. She was in a position to humiliate these rich folks who wronged her and would. It's just a little mischief she told herself. She will work to get the skirts separate from the blouse and expose backsides and would release stink bombs.

That night in disguise she went to the parade grounds. The gate was locked but not an issue. She picked locks. There was a guard she her didn't count on. She was dressed in beige catsuit to prevent being seen and blend with the tent. She trots and runs and stretch so it seems she is exercising. Once she grabs her legs looking through them to see if she's being followed. She hedged close to the fence and far spaced trees. The guard walked and checked the lock and moved to the other side. Before she could pick the lock, she heard a car and hid along the fence. It stopped and a voice called Gus. The guard answered. She went to the far side and with difficulty climbed the fence. The voice said he saw someone there. Gus assured him he was alone. She went in the tent and took out a pen light to bury the bombs she started to itch. She forgot to wear cotton. She cannot scratch she doesn't have room. She bent her toes, cross and rubbed her legs together. It didn't work. She has to forget it and do the bombs. She set the timer on two bombs then she heard the guard. She killed the light. There was a sound she heard it too. He swept the areas and she got flat face down. After he left, she heard him, 'it is you kitty.' The itch and nerves worked against her. It was hard to concentrate. Finally, she set the timer on the last one. She dropped dye in the hair sprays there. She eased her way out the tent. Gus seemed to be conversing with kitty. She reached up and was pulling herself when a voice says, ' Take my hand.' She knew the voice what is he doing here. She grabbed his hand and was over.

"Not a word," Rutherford said.

"Thank you." she said squirning.

"What's the matter with you? Why are you fidgeting."

"I'm itchy, I'm sensitive to synthetic material and I forgot my protection," she said.

"Go tell your mom bye. We are going to the airport," he said.

Maryanne showered and changed. How did Rutherford know where to find her. Does that mean others can too? Is he willing to listen to her or is he mad. But he said the airpot so he still wants to marry her. She hurried said good bye and left. They drove quickly and he went to her house dropped the car and they got a cab. She was exhausted and dozed. They checked in early and had cracker and hot chocolate. While she did cross word puzzles heread she a magazine. When they went aboard, she rests on his shoulders and slept. Zane picked them up. Due to emergency Liz went to work. The grandparent and grandchildren went to church however; breakfast was prepared for them. Liz came in after 3. pm and the usual family gathering happened.

The following day after breakfast the four of them went to see Rev Gilbert. Introductions were made more so, Rutherford. Maryanne he remembered having visited the church sometime past. He asked the relevant questions - views on marriage, monogamy, sanctity of the matrimonial bed, tolerance and acceptance of traditional vows or are they writing their own vows. The couple was ambivalent about writing their vows but, would notify him ahead of time. They agreed to a conference call before the wedding - seven days before. He asked them if anyone would have cause to stop their marriage; to think carefully of broken or forgotten promises. They assured him that would never happen. He prayed with them, blessed their engagement ring reminding them of the symbolism of the ring. They thanked the Minister and left.

Because Maryanne and Rutherford were leaving the next day decided to spend the day at the beach. Liz declined to join them, but told them to call when they were ready. She stayed away too long from Ethan. Later that evening Zoe had her love fest with her godmother, after homework. School would be out in another month or so, so she could spend more time with her godmother (so she thought). Maryanne forgot that she was to call her mother. It was Memorial Day! She called and got the news she expected, the costumes came apart at the waist leaving the leading ladies posterior hanging out. Poor Mrs Busch decided to a shape wear pad aka a butt lifter pads and when the skirt fell everyone saw it and laughed. Just the fact that the buttocks were out was hilarious and, to make matters worst some sort of odor was released. It smelled like rotten eggs. People scattered running from the scent. The ladies were scrambling to pull the skirts up front and back to hide their dignity. It was pandemonium! Then the journalists on spot snapping photos of the happening. We laughed so hard. You should have been there. Maryanne laughed and laughed. Buy me copies mom if they make the papers. She hung up grinning from ear to ear.

"We are on the 7:30 am flight tomorrow so we better go to bed early," said Maryanne.

Just before they turned in Liz said she hadn't listened to any news or weather report all day. They are able to get a number of US stations by satellite feed and just as she was about to change it she saw Memorial Day celebration and paused. She called Maryanne and Rutherford to come and look. There was Port Charlotte and the newscaster stated costume malfunction at one of the Memorial Day events. It showed briefly the dropped skirts and blurred buttocks. At the same event there was sort of release of some odor like rotten eggs. Police identified it as stink bombs, most likely placed there by pranksters. Maryanne laughed and laughed: " The leading ladies are exposed."

"You seem very pleased," remarked Rutherford to Maryanne

"What are you kidding? Only sorry I was not on hand to see it. That's magnificent! Magnifico indeed dear Ford. Magnifico indeed!"

Rutherford laughed and knew his fiancee was involved in it. Was that what she was doing Saturday night? He looked at her and wagged his finger."Ah-ha!"

"What's happening here. You know these people? Liz asked.

"You could say so. They are the elitists of our town. Oh boy! Oh boy. Mom just told me about it," said Maryanne.

"Okay guys. We have to get to the airport no later than 5,45 so it's early night for you, although you should sleep very well, said Liz. Turning to Zane, Are the children asleep?"

"Yes my honey," said Zane.

The weather report said rain in the east and chance of rain in the corporate area. Highs in the 90's . Stay hydrated.

They left and went to bed.

As Maryanne turned to put her shoes in her luggage, Rutherford entered the room.

"Tell me M A . The Port Charlotte calamity is that your handy work?"

"Didn't you hear the newscaster say possibly pranksters," she prevaricated.

"M A is that your project, he asked again so softly. You were so elated back there, it looked like triumph."

"Okay Rutherford. I promised I would tell you everything. Yes I rigged the costumes so they separate as well as plant the stink bombs. That's just my abnormal sense of justice, just to take them down a notch or two. The ultimate if it's captured on film. The imp of mischief goad me into doing it. I also helped fate with Matthew Busch, Chad Broome and Griffen Spoolson. My task was to make things uncomfortable and put them in the hot seat, create embarrassment. Yes I did it.bI found Caldren Forke and he's the only one that seems to have a conscience. He has remorse over what he did. The horse whipping his conscience giving him! He is broken and beaten. He is suffering so I walked away. Plus he's trying to make amends, make a difference through after school programs.m He speaks about right decisions and abstenance from alcohol, drugs, smoking and bad influence. So now you know everything," she ended.

He smiled and shook his head. "Thank you. I wanted you to trust me. We don't need secrets between us. Secrets you share with your sister does matter but this is different and crucial. I got the idea you might be involved because Chad Broome talked about meeting a red head who mysteriously disappeared - went in the bathroom and vanished. Your job as concierge nurse provides opportunities for you. So I started to give an eye for your security. I didn't like it the woman I love taking unnecessary risks."

"So you were spying on me?" she asked angrily.

"Keep your voice down. Not spying per se - making sure you were safe safe. How could I stand aside and let you take those risks. I was in Boston and I know that was you."

"How do you know?"

"I found the guys, followed them, follow you. You plant the catalyst for Spoolson and that literally closed him down. I told you about the cold case so you'd stop risking your life. I can't lose you. He pulled her in his arms. You have no idea how much I love you. So that being said you pulled your last prank. Cold case file is working . We have the proof we need. I promised when I changed major I'd do everything to get justice for you and bring those bastards. So, let us get married and deal with what's coming as man and wife. No more distance between us."

On June 5th the Cold case team and FBI Special Agents visited Port Charlotte and the precinct and Broome placed Chief under arrest for obstruction of justice and tampering with evidence. Similarly Reginald Busch with criminal conspiracy, tampering with evidence and bribery. Matt, Chad and Griffin were together licking their wounds when they were arrested. Rutherford had the pleasure of putting the handcuffs on Chad Broome and read him his rights. The others were arrested by other officers. It created a sensation. Print and electronic media had a a feeding frenzy. Once Caldren heard he took a flight to Port Charlotte and turned himself in. A call from Geneva encouraged him to be witness for the prosecution. They were arraigned and DA Ronald McNabb was pleased.m He was happy he was pursuaded to return to Port Charlotte six months ago.

Maryanne and Rutherford had their destination wedding. The weather was on its best behavior and the wedding was spectacular. Palm fronds, gardenias, anthuriums, ginger rose, bird bird of paradise, combined to create a thoroughly professional yet homey ambience. The diamond shaped fronds conspired with delicate lace that was ethereal; a feast for the eyes as while chairs with wild flowers held hands along the aisle. And the bride and groom a vision to behold - the Viking and the princess her voice sweet and dainty and his deep. There were sixty guests who ate freely of appetizers and entrees. The food was delicate and delectable and and hearty and rugged.

Everything and everyone was beautiful. Grams - Esther Norma Wood was beautiful thriving under the Jamaican sun and Clarice young and giddy for her daughter having a fantastic time with her two pals Beatrice and Joan. As the shadows lengthened Thriller Disc pulsed as the bridge and groom danced to And I Will Always Love You by Whitney Houston. Later others joined in. Amid the dancing the bridal bouquet was tossed and caught. The happy couple left for their honeymoon - a secret to the bride. And the guests continued to dance way into the wee hours of the morning.

It was August 10th and the re- trial for Rape Sexual Battery was brought against the infamous four. The parents' trial was later.

Judge Lesley Ann Sugar presided. There was a request for limited access trial in consideration for the victim and miscarriage of justice that happened previously. Media was blocked with the exception of Vanessa Postee WPNY Boston and Dee Parchment WSBN, family was admitted. This time was confident and prepared. However the star was witness for the prosecution. A gasp was heard and shock mirrored the faces. After he was sworn in he stated his name for the record. He was asked if he was pressured, threatened or in anyway way coerced to give testimony.

He stated he was not given any promises, or deals or reduced sentence. He was doing for conscience sake. He needed to be free.

The other defendants turned green. They were frazzled, obviously panicked. The Three lawyers conferred. They knew they lost; Caldren had nothing to gain. Surprise number two was Greg. He started talking two days ago and remembered the boys conversation. When the lawyers object they were told DA McNabb filed motion for special circumstances on the eve of previous trial he was hit and run victim. They want to make sure he was alive and healthy to testify. They were over ruled. The defense attorneys asked for a brief recess. They approached the DA. Maryanne said no deal. We have two witnesses, forensic evidence. We don't need them. This case is tighter than a goat skin over a drum. They entered no contest but without reduced sentence. Each had to serve mandatory ten years before eligible for parole with exception of Chad Broome. He got fifteen to thirty years - mandatory fifteen served before eligible for parole. In addition they had to state publicly they raped Maryanne Radieux.

Maryanne petition court for leniency for Caldren Forke: he didn't rape her but was complicit, embarked on changing lives his community work she had first on knowledge about. He volunteered to be witness without favor. Consequently two years and probation for three.

Epilogue

aryanne finally made her peace with Port Charlotte and she and Rutherford found a four bedrooms and three bathrooms. At the urging of Liz they start attending First Presbyterian Church of Port Charlotte. They need to work on their prayer life. God has been faithful to them and should find a church home. Anyway they might very well be treated as outcast in the church she used to attend. So they have been coming for a year. The young minister is very good and he gets better every week. They like the congregation. They are genuinely warm and friendly. They were asked to become members. When they told Liz she was ecstatic and urged them to become members especially now she decides she wants to be a mama. Both of them prayed. They needed the peace and tranquility of Liz and Zane and their quiet acceptance and belief in God and the gratitude they show. As Liz enthused about their decision she urged her to forgive the other three rapists. And go to God. Ask the Pastor Silver Winstar to help her. The couple asked and the pastor helped. They became members.

I baptize you in the name of the father, the Son and Holy Ghost intoned Pastor Silver Today we put off the old man as you emersed and raise with the living Christ. Maryanne held her breath as she was submerged in the Charlotte Dayton Beach. As she emerges and took a gulp of fresh air the assembled Church members cheered. It wasn't usually done but was nice. Next Rutherford was baptized. Their very public confession of Jesus as her Savior and Lord could not be more public. They requested emersion as in the ancient text and tradition signifying the death of sin and resurrection with Christ. She did not want any mistake neither did she ambiguity as to her position as a Christian. The members broke in Amazing Gracas they stood in full white. They changed in a make shift tent.

She had not reached this decision lightly, but once made was committed. Her walk with Christ must have meaning and the same dedication she had when she fostered hate, revenge and unforgiveness. There would be time for reflection but right now just want to bask in the lightness and glee she was feeling. As they looked along the horizon a double rainbow appeared. They praise God for the promise and the new life.

"We start a new life," said Rutherford.

"Yes, we do. All of us, she said quietly.

"Of course, honey. You and me, said Rutherford.

"And I agree, all of us," she said with a dreamy look. She reached for his hand and placed it on her stomach. Yes all of us.

Rutherford let out a whoop. He finally got it. And the members that it was the Holy Spirit until they saw him kissing his wife.

About the Author

Claudette H. McLennon is a migrant from Jamaica who settled in New York for many years. She is an avid reader of romance novels, mysteries, and spy thrillers. She has an intimate and long-standing love affair with books. She loves the Bible stories as well as the Hardy Boys stories told her by her siblings. This sparked a love for writing stories. Hence, this story is the lively imagination of a teenager translated and brought to life forty years later.

This love of writing also led to publishing Ode to Lillet Rose, a book of poetry, and her first novel Sins of the Parents (due 2022). Currently retired, she is committed to writing more novels/ poetry. When not working as part-time Mary Kay consultant, she enjoys listening to music, doing crossword puzzles, doodling, arts and crafts, and light cooking.